Katie
and the
Snow
Babies

Collect all six Arctica Mermaid books

Also look out for the six original Mermaid SOS adventures in Coral Kingdom

Katie and the Snow Babies

gillian shields

illustrated by helen Turner

BLOOMSBURY
CHILDREN'S
BOOKS

Follow the Arctica

Underwater
Volcano

Fire Isles

Wha

Beachcomber
Islands

The Big Waves

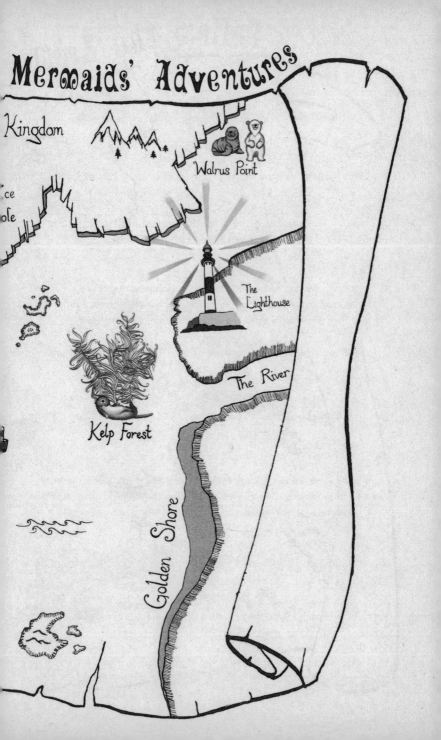

Mermaids' Adventures

Kingdom

Walrus Point

The Lighthouse

The River

Kelp Forest

Golden Shore

First published in Great Britain in 2007 by Bloomsbury Publishing Plc,
36 Soho Square, London, W1D 3QY

A CIP catalogue record of this book is available from the British Library

ISBN 978 0 7475 8975 4

Printed and bound in Great Britain by Clays Ltd, St Ives Plc

1 3 5 7 9 10 8 6 4 2

All papers used by Bloomsbury Publishing are natural, recyclable products
made from wood grown in well-managed forests. The manufacturing processes
conform to the environmental regulations of the country of origin.

For the lovely Simone
— G.S.

For the St. Mary's girls —
Katherine, Liz, Angela and Helen
— Love H.T.

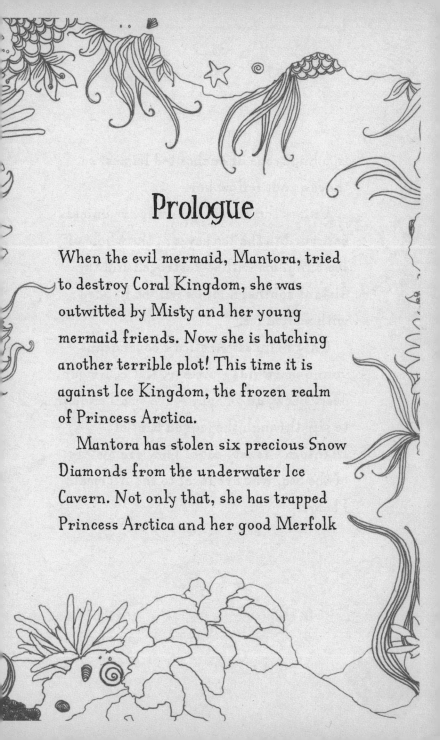

Prologue

When the evil mermaid, Mantora, tried
to destroy Coral Kingdom, she was
outwitted by Misty and her young
mermaid friends. Now she is hatching
another terrible plot! This time it is
against Ice Kingdom, the frozen realm
of Princess Arctica.

Mantora has stolen six precious Snow
Diamonds from the underwater Ice
Cavern. Not only that, she has trapped
Princess Arctica and her good Merfolk

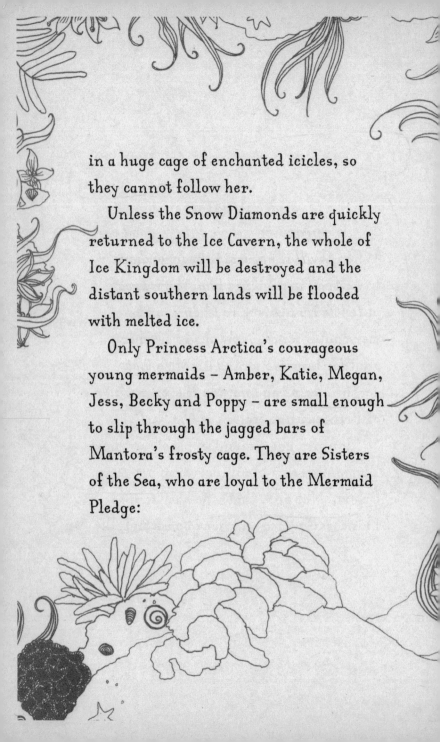

in a huge cage of enchanted icicles, so they cannot follow her.

Unless the Snow Diamonds are quickly returned to the Ice Cavern, the whole of Ice Kingdom will be destroyed and the distant southern lands will be flooded with melted ice.

Only Princess Arctica's courageous young mermaids – Amber, Katie, Megan, Jess, Becky and Poppy – are small enough to slip through the jagged bars of Mantora's frosty cage. They are Sisters of the Sea, who are loyal to the Mermaid Pledge:

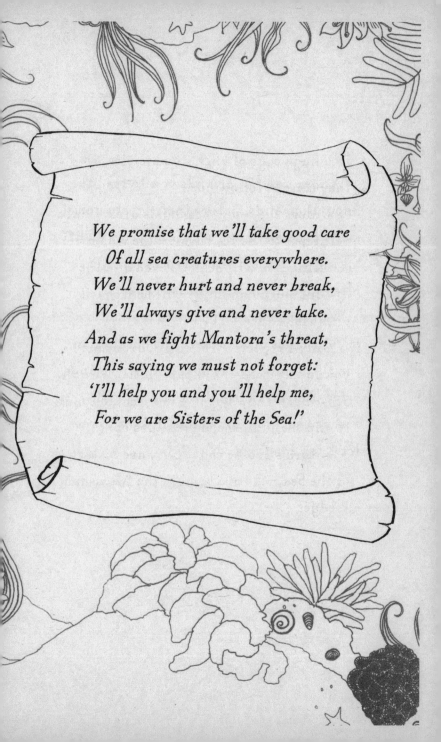

We promise that we'll take good care
Of all sea creatures everywhere.
We'll never hurt and never break,
We'll always give and never take.
And as we fight Mantora's threat,
This saying we must not forget:
'I'll help you and you'll help me,
For we are Sisters of the Sea!'

Amber and her friends vow to find the
Snow Diamonds, before their frosty home
melts for ever. They set off on their quest,
taking with them only Princess Arctica's
blessing and their Stardust Lockets.

Mantora has left behind a trail of
cryptic clues about where she has hidden
the Diamonds. Can Amber and her friends
solve Mantora's riddling rhymes and
rescue the Snow Diamonds in time to save
Ice Kingdom?

If you cannot find the Diamonds,
The ice will start to melt.
On all sides of the Ocean,
The danger will be felt.
No more will seals and polar bears
Enjoy their snowy home,
The seas will rise, the lands will flood —
Storm Kingdom will have come!
So try to solve the riddling clues
Of Mantora's cruel game,
But if you fail to work them out,
The world won't be the same ...

Katie

Chapter One

'What does it say, Amber?' asked Katie. The Sisters of the Sea were gathered on the ice, next to the cold, deep waves. Amber was holding a sinister purple parchment, covered with spidery black writing. It was a message from their enemy, Mantora, who had stolen and hidden the precious Snow Diamonds.

Katie and her brave young friends –

Amber, Megan, Jess, Becky and Poppy –
had vowed that they would find all the
Diamonds in time to save Ice Kingdom.
They had already found the first one when
they had rescued Benjy, a baby beluga
whale, from an underwater trap. Now
Benjy and his family were swimming
freely in the sparkling water that lapped
against the ice edge.

Amber looked up anxiously. 'It's the clue to find the second Snow Diamond,' she said. 'I'm too nervous to read it. Could you do it please, Katie?'

Katie pushed her long dark plait over her shoulder, smoothed out the parchment and began to read aloud:

'Where the kings of the ice
Meet the lords of the sea,
A Diamond falls from the sky –
Very strange, you'll agree!
So search high and low,
If you want to save your snow!'

'Mantora has written something else underneath,' she added.

19

'You may have found the first Diamond,

you little busy-bodies,

but it is useless without the other five.

I'm giving you a sporting chance to find the second one, though.

All you have to do is solve my riddle – fast!'

'Oh, this clue is so hard,' groaned Megan. 'Whatever does it mean – "*kings of the ice*" and "*lords of the sea*"?'

All the mermaids looked puzzled. Then Becky said shyly, 'My father says that the polar bear is the king of the ice. Does that help?'

'Polar bears!' said the others. 'Of course, they are stronger than any of the other creatures who roam the icy lands.'

'But what about the "*lords of the sea*"?' asked Jess, running her fingers through her dark curls. 'Whoever could they be?'

Benjy poked his friendly face above the waves and cried out, 'We're the lords of the sea, aren't we, Dad?'

His father looked up as he glided past.

'That's what we whales like to think, Benjy,' he said, blowing heavily. 'The walruses wouldn't agree, though. They think they are the finest creatures in the whole of Ice Kingdom!'

The young friends looked at each other uncertainly. Could the second clue be about the huge, stately walruses? They were surely splendid enough to be called lords.

'So perhaps we need to go where we can see polar bears and walruses together,' said Katie slowly. '"*Where the kings of the ice meet the lords of the sea*"…isn't that what it says?'

'The best place for that is Walrus Point,' said red-headed Poppy decidedly. 'I've heard that you often see polar bears near the icy headland where the walruses gather.'

'Then we'd better set off at once,' exclaimed Katie.

'…er, Katie,' murmured Megan nervously, 'haven't you forgotten that polar bears and walruses sometimes fight each other? They can be quite fierce, you know.'

Becky seemed rather worried, too.

'Aren't we prepared to risk anything, and face any danger, to solve the clues and save Ice Kingdom?' asked Katie, sitting up on her lemon-coloured tail and looking round solemnly at her young friends.

'Yes!' said brave, daring Jess.

'So am I,' said Amber seriously.

'Me too!' cried Poppy.

Becky and Megan held hands and

swallowed hard. 'Then so are we,' they promised. 'Let's go to Walrus Point!'

The mermaids hugged each other and got ready to dive into the icy waves, where the beluga whales still circled like sleek, white ships.

'How will you get there, Mermaids?' asked Benjy, looking up at his friends. 'Walrus Point is far away.'

'We'll just have to swim,' shrugged Jess, 'even if it takes a long time.' With a ripple of her strong turquoise tail, she slipped into the water next to him. Katie and the others followed her.

'But you need to find the Diamonds soon, or it will be too late,' said Benjy, a frown creasing his smooth little face. 'Can't we help them, Dad?'

Benjy's father swam closer to the mermaids.

'I'm afraid we are weak after being trapped for so long,' he sighed. 'We need to rest here and get our strength back. But we have a friend who might be able to help you.'

The belugas made their eerie cry, and

they were soon answered by a deep, echoing call. The clear blue water suddenly heaved, as though a powerful boat was cutting through the waves. In a few moments, a gigantic humpback whale raised his magnificent head above the surface of the sparkling sea.

'It's our friend Monty!' cried Benjy in delight. 'He'll take you anywhere you want to go, mermaids!'

'Oh, ho, ho, it's mermaid business, is it?' said Monty, with a wide smile. 'Just hop on my back,

little ones, and we'll be off straight away.
All aboard the Whale Express!'

Katie and her friends could hardly
believe this amazing piece of luck. Monty
was a strong, tireless whale who could
carry them all the way to Walrus Point
much faster than they could ever swim.

'Thank you so much!' cried the
mermaids. They clung on tightly to
Monty, as the huge whale plunged away
from the snowy shore.

'Goodbye, Benjy!' they called. 'We'll
bring the Snow Diamonds home very soon
– we promise.'

After what seemed like many hours of
surging through the icy sea, Monty called
out cheerfully, 'Here we are, Mermaids.
We've arrived!'

Katie and the others slid gracefully from Monty's broad back and rippled their tails in the clear waves. They gazed round and admired the frosty icebergs that towered above them like carved mountains, glinting with dusky purple shadows.

'This really is a wild and lonely part of Ice Kingdom,' said Katie. She checked that her shining Mermaid Harp was hanging safely at her side, then added, 'Where should we look for the walrus folk?'

'You need to swim towards the ice edge,' answered Monty. 'You will soon see them there. I will wait for you in these deep waters. It's time for the Whale Express to take a nap!'

And it was time for the Sisters of the Sea to search for the second Snow Diamond...

Chapter Two

The mermaids thanked Monty and
promised to return as quickly as they
could. Then Katie swished her glistening
tail and swam with her friends past the
looming, craggy icebergs. Very soon, they
reached the ice edge. It was a long, white,
frosty shore, where the flat frozen plains
met the sea. At the far end of the shore,
jutting out into the water, was a headland

made of tumbled blocks of ice. A few sea birds wheeled above the broken cliffs in the bright, cold sky.

'That headland must be Walrus Point, where the walrus folk gather,' said Jess.

'Wait!' called Katie, as Jess and the others began to surge towards it. 'Let's sit on the edge of the ice for a moment, and decide what to say to them. The walrus folk can be very quick-tempered sometimes. We don't want to upset them.'

With a twist of their tails, the young friends pulled themselves out of the water, and sat on the sparkling snow.

'I'm a bit worried about meeting the walruses,' confessed Megan. 'Their long tusks sometimes look a bit scary.' She carefully tucked her pet Fairy Shrimp,

Sammy, deeper into her cosy pocket.
Sammy had been given special powers by a
Stardust sprinkle, which meant that he
could breathe out of water and follow the
mermaids everywhere. But Megan didn't
want him to be squashed by a rough,
tough walrus.

'Don't worry,' said Amber. 'If we are
polite and respectful, I'm sure we won't
have any problems. But tell Sammy to
keep out of sight until we're sure that they
are friendly.'

'I hope we're right that the "*lords of the
sea*" in the clue really are the walrus folk,
now that we have come all this way,' said
Becky.

'And that the "*kings of the ice*" are the
polar bears,' added Jess.

'I'm sure we are right about that, but "*diamonds falling from the sky*" is just silly!' interrupted Poppy cheekily. 'I think Mantora must be completely potty.'

'No, she isn't,' said Amber, gravely shaking her golden curls. 'Mantora might enjoy taunting us with her fiendish clues, but she is deadly serious about hiding the

Snow Diamonds away for ever, so that Ice Kingdom will melt.'

'And you must take our quest seriously as well,

Poppy,' said Katie, with a small sigh.

'I know, I know,' said Poppy breezily. 'You don't need to give me a lecture. I want to find the Diamonds just as much as you do.'

As the mermaids were talking, they didn't notice a large, blue shadow creeping across the ice behind them…

'We're all on the same side in this battle,' urged Megan. 'We should put our energy into solving Mantora's clue, not quarrelling!'

The dusky shadow grew nearer…

'You're right,' said Katie. 'So what could the clue mean? Whoever heard of a Snow Diamond falling from the sky?'

For a moment the mermaids were silent, puzzling over the strange riddle.

The shadow stopped moving.

'Perhaps…this may be wrong, of course,' Becky hesitated. 'But what about a shooting star? They are as bright and beautiful as a diamond, and they seem to fall through the sky.'

'Well, it's a start,' replied Katie slowly. 'Let's find the walruses and ask them if there have been any shooting stars here lately.'

'And remember,' added Amber, 'we must ask nicely. No being cheeky, Poppy!'

'I'm not frightened of any old walrus,' Poppy boasted. 'Or of any "*kings of the ice*" either. So there!'

The blue shadow suddenly quivered into life. The mermaids heard a deep growl behind them.

'Not afraid of the kings of the ice?' thundered a wild, rasping voice. 'Oh, but you should be afraid. Very afraid!'

Katie and her friends whipped round in horror, and saw a terrifying sight. A huge, shaggy polar bear was rearing up on its paws behind them. He really was the King of the Ice, and he was getting ready to pounce...

'Stop!' gasped Katie, with trembling lips. 'Don't hurt my friends!'

The enormous polar bear dropped back on to all four paws and stared at the mermaids clutching on to each other. He sniffed and snorted and then...he smiled.

'Of course I won't hurt you,' he said apologetically. 'Allow me to introduce myself. My name is Finn.'

At that moment, a plump ball of white
fluff poked his head round Finn's heavy
legs and grinned at the mermaids. It was a
baby polar bear.

'And don't forget me,' he squeaked.

'Mermaids,' said Finn, with a low bow.
'Meet my son, Max.'

'But…but…' wondered Katie, 'why did
you frighten us like that, Finn?'

'To show you how easy it is for careless
talk to be overheard,' replied the father

polar bear, with a deep rumble in his throat. 'I could have been Mantora creeping up on you, and then where would you have been?'

Katie and the others looked at each other with concerned faces. They hadn't thought of that. It would be terrible if Mantora sneaked up and overheard their plans, or even worse, captured them with one of her dark Storm spells.

'It's true,' admitted Jess. 'We were being

careless, Finn, and you were right to teach us a lesson.'

'Dad's always right!' cried Max happily. Then he did a roly-poly into the circle of mermaids, tumbling over their tails and ending up on Megan's lap. The young friends couldn't help laughing delightedly. They took turns to give Max cuddles and stroke his soft, white fur.

'But do you know anything about the missing Snow Diamond, Finn?' asked Katie, tearing herself away from the baby bear's games. 'Have you seen one falling from the sky?'

Finn shook his powerful head. 'I heard what you said about Mantora's clue. I roam far over the wide ice, and I have also heard rumours that she has been plotting against Princess Arctica. But this clue of hers makes no sense to me at all. You'll have to ask Ulrick.'

'Who is Ulrick?' chorused the others, looking up from their little playmate.

'Ulrick is the Chief Walrus,' said Finn. 'He's the wisest creature in these parts. He's also the most proud, stubborn and annoying!'

Finn sat down heavily on the powdery

snow and rested his head on his paws. His dark eyes stared moodily into the distance.

'So you're not friends?' Becky asked timidly. 'You can't take us to see him?'

'Friends!' barked Finn, with a throaty growl. 'We used to be the best of friends. But we had a silly quarrel about who was the strongest and wisest, and it turned into a stupid fight. I tried to make it up with him afterwards, but Ulrick wouldn't listen. He won't even let Max here play with his baby grandson, Caspar.'

Max stopped cuddling Poppy for a moment and looked up sadly.

'Caspar is my friend,' he said. 'I want to see him.'

'Not today, Max,' said Finn gloomily. 'Maybe another time.' The father bear hung his head over his little son and nuzzled him softly. 'But this isn't helping you, Sisters of the Sea,' he added, suddenly snapping out of his sorrowful mood. 'Go and visit Ulrick straight away, to ask if he can help you with this clue. You must find the Diamond and save our snowy home.'

The mermaids quickly roused themselves. They gave Max one last kiss, then slipped from the ice into the clear waves, with a splash of their sparkling tails.

'It might cause trouble if I come with you,' said Finn. 'Swim along by the ice edge until you reach the headland at Walrus Point. Ulrick and his folk bathe in the water there every day. Good luck!'

In a flash of rainbow colours –

turquoise, lemon, blue, peach, pink and lilac – the mermaids darted under the cold sea. They felt sorry that Finn and Ulrick were no longer friends, and rather nervous about meeting the Chief Walrus himself. But the only thing that mattered now was trying to solve the clue...

Chapter Three

As Katie and her friends swam closer to Walrus Point, they saw several powerful sea creatures twisting and turning in the water ahead. They had found the walruses!

'Excuse me,' Poppy asked boldly. 'We're looking for Ulrick.'

A walrus mother glided near to the mermaids. 'You mean *Lord* Ulrick, my dear. He's Overwater right now, sunning himself on the big blocks of ice that stick out into the sea at the headland. Swim straight up if you want to speak to him – but mind your manners!'

The mermaids followed the direction of the mother walrus's pointing flipper, and surged above the waves. They hovered for a moment near the headland.

'There he is!' whispered Becky.

Above them on the ice, surrounded by his loyal folk, was the magnificent Chief Walrus. His splendid brown chest gleamed in the sun, and his long whiskers and immense tusks added to his stately dignity.

'Um…greetings, Ulrick, I mean *Lord* Ulrick,' Katie called up politely. 'We have come here on a very important mission, seeking your wise advice.'

The Chief Walrus peered down his long tusks to where the mermaids bobbed up and down below him in the green sea. A group of heavy walruses gathered clumsily next to him on the ice so that they could listen and watch. Ulrick cleared his throat slowly, then spoke in a rich, rolling voice.

'It is true that I am the wisest creature in these parts,' he said grandly. 'You may tell me your tale, but swiftly! The Chief Walrus cannot waste his time.'

Katie hurriedly explained all about the theft of the Snow Diamonds and Mantora's taunting clues.

'So we thought the Diamond falling

from the sky might be a shooting star,'
Poppy burst in impatiently. 'Do you think
we're right?'

The Chief Walrus stared down at
Poppy's mop of copper curls.

'It is not our way to say "yes" or "no" in
the blink of an eye, like a giddy shrimp,'
he said disapprovingly. Sammy the Fairy
Shrimp popped his head out of Megan's
pocket. Was this old fellow talking about
him? Then he dived out of sight again,
alarmed by the sight of Ulrick's bristling
moustache.

'Besides,' the noble walrus continued,
'how could one single mermaid cause so
much trouble? Now, if it was a rascally
polar bear who wanted to take over Ice
Kingdom, I could well believe it. But a

mere *mermaid*? Whoever heard of such a thing!'

He and his walruses began to laugh in a deep, rippling rumble that echoed like thunder over the wide plains of ice. Katie glanced at the other mermaids in dismay. She hadn't expected this! On all sides, the massive brown creatures were rolling helplessly with mirth, clutching their smooth sides with their waving flippers.

'But Mantora really is powerful…' Katie tried to explain hurriedly.

The Chief Walrus suddenly stopped laughing. He held himself straight and quivered with pride.

'No one has any power over what happens in Walrus Point except the Chief Walrus,' he declared, banging his flipper down hard on the frosted ice.

'But if we don't get the Snow Diamonds back, the whole of Ice Kingdom will melt – yes, even Walrus Point!' said Poppy angrily, swimming in front of the other mermaids. She stared up fearlessly into the Chief Walrus's stern face. 'And it's no good pretending that it won't happen.'

Becky and Megan gasped and held hands in the water, as Katie looked round

at her friends with worried eyes. The
walruses would never help them with the
clue if Poppy annoyed their leader! But
Katie knew in her heart that what Poppy
said was right. The Chief Walrus,
however, didn't like it one little bit.

'How dare you speak to me in this way?'
Ulrick glared, his whiskers shaking with
disbelief.

'Because it's the truth,' Poppy declared.

Katie swam right up to the ice edge,
took a deep breath and said, 'Poppy
doesn't mean to be cheeky, sir. I'm afraid

she is right about the Diamonds. Finn told
us you were wise and would know what to
do…'

But she never got the chance to finish
her sentence. Ulrick rose up on his flippers
and his face grew dark with rage.

'Finn?' he bellowed. 'You have spoken to
that no-good polar bear? Well, you foolish
young creatures, let me tell you that any
friend of Finn is no friend of mine. Be off

with you at once,
and take your silly
tales of melting
icebergs with you!'

He turned and
waddled slowly
away from the ice
edge, turning his

back on the shocked mermaids. Everything was going very wrong, thought Katie. She had to do something – and she had to do it quickly.

With a sharp flick of her lemon-coloured tail, Katie pulled herself out of the sea and on to the ice.

'Lord Ulrick! Please wait,' she gasped. The others quickly followed her on to the frosty headland. But at that moment, the mermaids heard a sudden noise of wailing and crying. It was coming from where the mother walruses were huddled together on the flat stretches of ice.

'Caspar! Oh, my lovely son, Caspar,' sobbed a plump mother walrus, as she scrambled clumsily over the ice towards Ulrick. The Chief Walrus spun his heavy head around towards her.

'Why are you weeping, Inga, my daughter?' he asked anxiously. 'What has happened to my dear grandson, Caspar?'

Inga paused and hid her face with her front flipper.

'My baby has gone,' she cried. 'We can't find him anywhere!'

The Chief Walrus's face seemed to grow haggard in front of the mermaids' eyes.

'G-g-gone,' he stammered. 'What do you mean?'

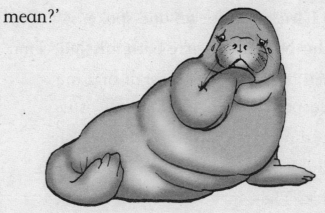

Then a rough, growly voice called out in answer from the sea, 'I can tell you, if you will listen.'

Katie, the mermaids and all the walrus folk swung round to see who was speaking. Paddling furiously through the waves towards the icy headland was a large, wet polar bear. It was Finn. He soon heaved himself out of the water and on to the ice, shaking his furry coat and scattering rainbow drops everywhere. Then he looked into Ulrick's dark eyes and spoke.

'Our babies – they're both missing,' Finn sighed heavily. 'Your Caspar and my Max!'

Chapter Four

Katie listened in shock as deep cries of concern echoed around the walrus folk. Ulrick stared at the father polar bear with a bewildered air. 'H-h-how can this be?' he stuttered.

Finn sat down wearily. 'Max and I had been talking with these brave mermaids,' he explained. 'Then we set off across the ice to go home. Max was dashing about

and playing as usual. But when I reached
our lair he wasn't with me any more. His
mother is sick with worry.'

'And Caspar has gone from our home,
too,' cried Inga.

Katie thought quickly. 'Finn,' she said,
turning to the father polar bear, 'didn't
you say that Max and Caspar were
friends? Couldn't they have
gone off together?' Then
she turned to Ulrick. 'You
wouldn't allow them to
play together, so they had
to sneak off without
telling their
families. Your
quarrel has put
them in danger.'

Ulrick hung his head in shame.

'You said that I was wise, Sisters of the Sea, but I see now that I have been so foolish,' he said humbly. 'Oh, Finn, my old friend, how could I let our stupid quarrel stand in the way of our babies' friendship?'

'It was a black day when our own friendship was broken,' answered Finn quietly. 'But maybe it is not too late to mend it.'

Ulrick looked up with hope in his eyes. 'I wanted to make up with you long ago,' he said, 'but I was too proud. And now our precious babies are lost in the wild snow – all because of my false pride.'

'Then let us forgive and forget,' said Finn gruffly. 'In the name of friendship, let us work together to get them back!'

The lordly walrus and the kingly polar bear solemnly embraced each other, good friends once more.

'And now,' said the Chief Walrus, 'we must put aside all that has happened in the past. Mermaids, I was wrong about Finn. Perhaps I was wrong about Mantora, too. But I cannot put my mind to those weighty matters until our young ones are found.'

'Will you help us to search for them,
Sisters of the Sea?' asked Inga, with
pleading eyes. Katie, Amber, Jess, Megan,
Becky and Poppy nodded in agreement.

'We'll help you,' they vowed. 'We'll do
everything we can to rescue your lost
babies.'

'But we need to have a plan,' added
Amber urgently. All the mermaids knew
that it would be difficult for the young
creatures to survive alone in the icy
wilderness, away from their families.

'Let's split up,' suggested Katie, looking
round at the creatures sitting expectantly
on the frosty headland. 'That way we
won't all be searching in the same place at
once.'

'Good idea, Katie,' said Jess. 'Finn could

search over the ice. Max and Caspar might be wandering far on the frozen plains.'

The shaggy polar bear rose quickly on to his strong paws.

'I will call my brothers to help me hunt for them,' said Finn, raising his head and uttering a deep roar. After a few moments, two other large polar bears bounded into view across the sparkling ice. They hesitated when they saw the Chief Walrus, and looked uncertainly at their brother,

Finn. But Ulrick spoke up.

'You are welcome,' he said. 'There is no longer any quarrel between the walrus folk and the bears. Speed on your way across the ice and good luck in your hunt!'

Finn and his brother bears set off swiftly across the wide, level ice, their white coats soon blending in with the horizon of snow.

'Could your folk swim up and down by the ice shore, looking for the little ones?' Megan asked Ulrick. He waved his flipper at several large walruses as a signal. They instantly dived into the sea to search by the frozen coast.

'And the sea birds could help us, too, if Katie calls them with her Harp,' suggested Becky.

Katie quickly lifted her delicate

Mermaid Harp from the cord over her
shoulders. She began to play a lively tune
on its golden strings. The sweet, wild notes
rose into the cloudless air. Before long,
there was a flutter of wings, and a group
of black and white guillemots landed on
the ice. Katie explained hurriedly what she
needed them to do.

'Will you seek far and wide over the cold
sea, and fly swiftly to tell us any news?'
she asked.

'We will!' the birds cried huskily, as
they flapped their strong wings and glided
away.

'And now we must go, too,' Katie
explained to Ulrick and Inga. 'We are
going to swim far from the ice shore to
search the open sea. Wait here for us, and

we will do our best to find them!'

One by one, the mermaids dived gracefully from the ice edge, calling their rescue cry: *Mermaid SOS!*

As the friends plunged underwater, hundreds of silver bubbles streamed out behind them. Swishing their jewelled tails, they darted away through the deep sea, calling 'M-a-x!' and 'C-a-s-par!' over and over again. But there was no reply.

'Be careful,' shouted Jess, who was slightly in front of the others. 'Iceberg ahead!'

Katie looked up and saw the craggy

65

sides of a huge underwater iceberg looming over her. The mermaids surged around it, carefully avoiding its sharp, menacing edges.

'There are lots of icebergs in this part of the sea,' said Amber.

'And lots of smaller ice floes too,' replied Becky thoughtfully, pointing upwards to the surface. The mermaids could see several chunks of ice floating above them on the waves, like frozen rafts.

'Have you noticed something else?' asked Poppy. 'The water doesn't seem as cold as it usually is. And some of those ice floes above us have strange cracks running across them.'

The mermaids looked up curiously.

'Let's go up to the surface and take a

quick peep,' said Katie. 'There's no sign of Max and Caspar down here anyway.'

As the young friends lifted their heads above the waves and shook their shining curls, they saw several jagged white ice floes. These flat lumps of ice jostled into each other on the surface of the swirling sea, like the muddled pieces of a jigsaw.

'You're right, Poppy,' said Megan. 'These blocks of ice are starting to break up. That must mean the water really is getting warmer!'

The young friends looked very concerned, as they hovered in the clear waves. Was this cracking ice just due to chance, or was it something to do with the missing Diamonds? Was Mantora's evil plan to let Ice Kingdom melt starting to work already?

'We've simply got to find those Snow Diamonds,' said Amber in a determined voice.

'But first, we've got to find those Snow Babies,' cried Katie. 'Caspar! Max! Are you out there?'

Chapter Five

The mermaids called the names of the
young creatures as loudly as they could.
Then they swam further out to sea,
weaving between the glistening ice floes
and the tips of the sparkling icebergs. All
the time they were calling and searching,
searching and calling. But it was no use.

'Ooof! I'm getting tired,' confessed
Megan after a while, her spangled pink

and white tail drooping in the water.

'So am I,' agreed Becky reluctantly.

'Let's stop for a moment,' suggested Katie. 'We can rest on one of the ice floes and decide what to do next.'

The friends thankfully chose a large block of ice that was floating near them like a raft, and gracefully wriggled on to it. Soon they were all sitting with their

glittering tails hanging down into the water and the breeze blowing in their hair.

'Look!' cried Jess, pointing up into the clear sky. 'The guillemots are swooping over to us. I hope they are coming to tell us that the babies have been found.'

But the sea birds wheeled over the mermaids' heads and called out that there was no news of Max or Caspar.

'So Finn hasn't found them on the ice, and the walruses haven't found them by the shore...' began Megan sadly.

'...and we can't see them anywhere underwater, or on the surface of the sea,' continued Becky.

'Perhaps they really are lost for good,' whispered Amber.

The mermaids held hands, feeling very

sad and worried. Katie began to sing
softly:

> *'Our mermaid song*
> *This message sends –*
> *We want to help*
> *Two special friends…'*

The others joined in, murmuring quietly:

> *'We want to help*
> *Two special friends…'*

Then a faint sound came floating back to
the mermaids on the wind.

'I can hear something!' said Katie. She
listened intently, cupping her hand round
her ear.

'What can you hear?' asked Megan hopefully.

Katie screwed up her face and strained to listen. 'It's someone calling,' she exclaimed.

The mermaids dived into the waves without a second's delay, racing in the direction of the distant voices. Very soon, they reached a small ice floe that was drifting dangerously fast. It was being dragged out to the open sea by the strong, swirling currents.

Peering over the edge of this frozen white raft were two scared little faces – a fluffy baby polar

73

bear and a plump
baby walrus!

The mermaids sped
forward and crowded
round them.

'You found us,
Katie,' murmured
Max, smiling weakly at his mermaid
friends. 'We heard your music and tried to
answer. But we're so tired and hungry
after clinging to this
ice for so long.'

'Let's get you home
and find out what
happened later,' said
Katie brightly. 'Can
you swim with us?'

'I c-can't swim,'

cried Caspar. 'I'm so cold and tired!'

'Oh, you poor thing,' said Megan gently. 'We'll help you to swim home somehow. But we must all hurry back to tell your families that you are safe.'

'We've got important business with Mantora to sort out, too,' added Poppy. 'And a clue to solve!'

Just as Katie was wondering how they were going to get the youngsters home, Amber remembered the bag that their friend Ana, the little Inuit girl, had given to them. It was tied loosely round her waist.

'Ana said this bag contained things we might need,' said Amber, rummaging around and lifting out some plaited ropes.

'I'm sure we could use those ropes to

help,' said Becky. 'Perhaps Max and Caspar could hold on to them, whilst we pull them along behind us?'

'B-b-but I might let go of it and s-s-sink,' said Caspar, with chattering teeth. The fright of his adventure had shaken him up.

'You won't sink if we give you a special touch of Stardust Magic,' said Katie kindly. 'Don't worry, Snow Babies.'

She strummed her golden Harp and chanted:

'Stardust, Stardust,
Make them float,
Turn these ropes
Into a boat,
Stardust, Stardust,

Make them ride
Over the waves,
Safe by our side!'

A stream of glittering sprinkles swooshed out of the mermaids' silvery Lockets and clung to the ropes. The long supple plaits began to coil and curl themselves round the Snow Babies, looping and twisting until Max and Caspar were sitting in two little basket-boats. The boats glowed with Stardust sprinkles, which would protect the young creatures from sinking.

'Come on, Snow Babies, you're going to have the ride of your lives!' laughed Katie.

The mermaids gently towed Caspar and Max through the greeny-blue waves, in their magical boats. The guillemots swooped and swirled overhead, and the young friends sang as they pulled the babies along:

> *'Our mermaid song*
> *This message sends –*
> *We have found*
> *Two special friends...'*

Soon, they all arrived at Walrus Point, where Ulrick and Inga were waiting anxiously for them.

Katie and the others carefully pulled themselves and the youngsters out of the water, until they all sat thankfully on the rough headland once more. The ropes slithered back to normal and Amber

carefully stowed them away in her bag.

Ulrick was overjoyed to see Caspar and Max, and Inga covered her son with walrus kisses.

'But how did you manage to get so far to sea?' wondered Katie.

Max cuddled up to the mermaids and explained, 'I wanted to see Caspar so I ran off to find him. We sneaked down to the ice edge to play without anyone seeing us. Then we met a mermaid lady, like you, but not so pretty. And she was bossy!'

'That must have been Mantora!' gasped Jess.

'She makes trouble wherever she is,' said Katie grimly. 'What happened next, Max?'

'The mermaid lady said it would be fun

for us to float on the ice floes, so we did,' Max continued. 'But they started to melt and break up. The piece of ice we were sitting on got swept out to sea on the currents.'

'I was so scared, but I feel better now,' said Caspar. 'I loved riding in that boat made of magical ropes! And I'm so glad to see you, Grandpa.'

The Chief Walrus hugged his baby grandson tenderly. Then he turned to the mermaids.

'We can never thank you enough, Sisters of the Sea,' he said. 'But young Max's tale shows that what you told us about Mantora's evil plot to melt the ice is true. I am so sorry that I ever doubted you.' He looked at Poppy with a twinkle in his eye.

'As for you, my dear, you are bold indeed,' he said. 'Bold enough to speak the truth to the Chief Walrus! I beg your pardon for not believing your wise words.'

Poppy grinned cheerfully. 'That's all right,' she said.

'My mother taught me that saying sorry for a mistake is the best wisdom of all, Lord Ulrick,' said Katie, in a serious voice.

The Chief Walrus bowed graciously, and continued, 'If those ice floes are starting to melt and break up, our lands really must be getting warmer. You must find the second Diamond without any further delay, before more damage is done!'

Chapter Six

Just as Katie was about to reply, a deep, happy roar rose from the sea and deafened the mermaids. Finn was swimming frantically through the waves towards the snowy shore. He leapt out of the water, scrambled up the ice edge and threw himself at Max. They tumbled over and over in a wild bear hug.

'Oh, Max,' he barked joyfully. 'I couldn't

find you on the ice, so I was searching in the water. I thought you had drowned, but now I've found you again. Your mother will be so happy when I take you home.'

'And it's all because of the mermaids,' Max smiled.

Finn turned to thank them, but first he shook his shaggy coat as usual, to dry his fur. The air was filled with diamond drops of water, like a sudden shower of…

'*Rain!*' exclaimed Katie, sitting up on her pearly tail in excitement. 'That's it! I understand now!'

'What do you mean?' asked Amber.

'It's in the clue – "*A diamond falls from the sky*",' she smiled. 'The diamonds falling from the sky are raindrops!'

The mermaids looked at Katie

hopefully. She clasped her hands together and turned pleadingly to the Chief Walrus.

'Ulrick,' she said, 'I know the rain doesn't often fall over these icy lands. But you *must* tell me if it has rained here lately. Our quest for the second Snow

Diamond might depend on it.'

Ulrick leaned forward on his strong flippers and gave Katie an astonished look, his moustache twitching in surprise.

'Why, yes,' he said in a puzzled voice. 'Only last night we had a most unexpected shower of rain here at Walrus Point. In fact, it was more than a shower of rain – it was a storm.'

The mermaids gathered round him on the rough ice, curling their glistening tails underneath them. 'Tell us what happened,' they begged.

'As we were settling to sleep on this icy headland,' said the Chief Walrus, 'some heavy black clouds sprang up in the sky from nowhere. The wind howled round us, sounding like weeping voices. Strange yellow light flooded over the snow, and we were battered with a storm of thick, icy hailstones.'

'That must have been Mantora's doing,' exclaimed Amber and Jess together.

'It certainly didn't seem natural,' shivered Ulrick. 'Even I felt a flicker of fear, as the sound of weeping turned into a menacing cackle of laughter. Then the storm stopped as suddenly as it began.'

'Now you see how powerful Mantora is,'

said Poppy. 'Only she could have made
that storm, with her dark magic.'

'But why would she do such a thing?'
asked Finn, in his deep growl.

'I think I understand,' said Becky quietly.
'Hailstones are frozen rain. They are lumps
of ice with a stone at their centre…'

'…and one of Mantora's enchanted
hailstones contained the Diamond instead
of a stone,' finished Katie. 'That's how the
Snow Diamond fell from the sky – inside a
frozen raindrop. It fell on to this headland
and is now buried under the snow!'

Everyone murmured in astonishment.

'So now we have to find exactly where
the Diamond fell down and buried itself,'
said Amber, gazing around eagerly. 'But it
could take for ever to find it.'

'No, it won't,' said a small, snuffly voice. 'Is this what you are looking for?' Caspar the baby walrus scrabbled in the ice near his grandfather. Then he waddled forward, looking bashful.

'I found a glittery stone after the horrid storm,' he explained. 'It was wrapped up in this red paper. I wanted to keep it, because it was so shiny. So I hid the stone and the paper back in the snow, right here where I always sit next to Grandpa. But you can have it, for saving me and my best friend, Max.'

He let the Diamond fall from his soft flipper on to Katie's outstretched hand. It flashed in the sun with every colour of the rainbow, but at its heart a white flame burned like a living icicle. Next to it was a small, blood-red scroll.

'Oh, well done, Caspar,' cried the mermaids in delight, petting him gratefully. Max rolled over in a bundle of white fluff to say 'Brilliant!' to his blushing friend.

Katie gave the scroll to Megan to look after whilst she showed the dazzling jewel to Ulrick, Finn and Inga.

'We've found the second Snow Diamond at last,' she said, 'thanks to you and the Snow Babies!'

'And now those babies must go home after the day's adventures,' said Finn. 'Come on, Max. Your mother will be longing to see you.'

'Can I play with Caspar tomorrow, Dad?' asked Max hopefully.

Finn glanced at his old friend. 'What does the Chief Walrus say?' he asked, with a faint smile.

'Of course you can, Max,' replied Ulrick heartily. 'Tomorrow, and the next day, and the day after that…'

'Hooray!' cried the two young friends. 'And hooray for the Mermaids!'

Katie and her friends laughed and cuddled Caspar and Max for one last time. Then they said goodbye to Ulrick and Inga, and last of all to Finn.

'Goodbye, Sisters of the Sea,' he said. 'You have done so much for us. The walrus folk and the polar bears will always be grateful. May you meet with good fortune on your quest – for all our sakes.'

The mermaids watched their friends

making their way across the ice to their homes. They had found two precious Snow Diamonds, but there was still a long and difficult task ahead of them before Ice Kingdom was truly safe.

'I think it's time to look at that scroll, Megan,' said Katie, turning to the others. 'Let's see what Mantora has dreamed up for us next.'

Megan squeezed Katie's hand quickly. 'Whatever it is, we're ready for it,' she said bravely. 'Aren't we, everyone?'

Katie, Amber, Jess, Becky and Poppy nodded their heads firmly. They were all ready to do their best to save their beloved Ice Kingdom. But the next stage of the quest wasn't going to be easy for the Sisters of the Sea...

Amber has golden curls and a gleaming lilac tail. She looks after her friends, and is a good leader.

Katie enjoys playing her Mermaid Harp. She has a long plait over her shoulder and a sparkly lemon-coloured tail.

Megan has sweet wavy hair and a spangled pink and white tail. She is never far from her pet Fairy Shrimp, Sammy.